DESTRO'S PLAN

by Michael Teitelbaum
based on the story by Michael Gordon and Stuart Beattie & Stephen Sommers
and the screenplay by Stuart Beattie and David Elliot & Paul Lovett
illustrated by Shane L. Johnson and Dan Panosian

Ready-to-Read

Simon Spotlight
New York London Toronto Sydney

Based on Hasbro's G.I. JOE® Characters

SIMON SPOTLIGHT
An imprint of Simon & Schuster Children's Publishing Division
1230 Avenue of the Americas, New York, New York 10020

Manufactured in the United States of America
2 3 4 5 6 7 8 9 10
ISBN: 978-1-4169-7852-7
LCCN 2008035908

CHAPTER ONE

Destro McCullen was not happy. He stood in the control room of the Pit, the top secret headquarters of the elite international military organization known as G.I. JOE.

Of course he was only present as a hologram, but to General Hawk, leader of the G.I. JOE team, and Duke, Ripcord, Scarlett, and the other soldiers, Destro was as real as any other person in the room.

Destro was the manufacturer of a new type of weapon that used nanomite technology. Nanomites were incredibly tiny machines that could be programmed to do anything.

He had sold these nanomite weapons to NATO. However, when these weapons were being delivered to NATO several days earlier, Destro himself had arranged for a team to steal the weapons.

But members of G.I. JOE had stopped Destro's unit, and brought the weapons to the Pit.

No one knew that Destro was the mastermind behind the plan to steal the weapons. Destro made sure this fact was kept a secret from General Hawk and the others.

"I spent ten years and billions creating these nanomite weapons," Destro said. "I'm glad your soldiers were able to save them, General."

"I'm not sure how those enemy agents learned about the weapons shipment," General Hawk said.

"That mission was classified," Duke added. "Yet someone knew exactly where the weapons would be."

"Well, you can be sure that they'll be safe here in the Pit," said General Hawk.

"So can I count on you to deliver the weapons to NATO now?" Destro asked.

"I think it would be best if we waited until we found and captured the agents who tried to steal them," the general replied.

"Very well," Destro said before turning away. He had a strange, satisfied look on his face.

CHAPTER TWO

Destro turned off the holographic cameras in his underwater base. He hurried to the base's main laboratory, ready to set his latest plan into motion.

In the lab, Destro joined the Doctor, a brilliant scientist who worked hard on perfecting nanomite technology.

Together, Destro and the Doctor had used the nanomites to make new superweapons. And the Doctor had yet another use for the nanomites.

"By injecting the nanomites into these men, I have created perfect soldiers," the Doctor explained. Behind him, rows of soldiers stood at attention. "I call them Neo Vipers."

"Perfect soldiers?" Destro asked curiously.

"Yes," the Doctor replied. "Because of the nanomites in them, they feel no fear and no pain. And they follow orders without question. Watch!"

The Doctor brought out an eighteen-foot-long cobra in a glass case. Then, punching several keys on a handheld device, the Doctor programmed a Viper soldier to put his hand into the snake case.

Without question, the soldier shoved his hand in and was immediately bitten by the cobra.

“You see? No fear, no pain,” the Doctor said when the Viper pulled his hand out. “The venom from a king cobra is strong enough to bring down an elephant.”

Then the Viper fell to one knee as the deadly venom attacked his body. A few seconds later, the Viper returned to standing at attention, his face calm.

“The nanomites in his blood battled the venom and defeated it,” the Doctor explained.

“Excellent,” Destro said. “Well done, Doctor.”

The following day, Destro gathered his team together. Leading the unit was Ana, a clever and deadly agent. Joining her was Storm Shadow, a highly skilled ninja, and a group of Neo Vipers.

"Thanks to General Hawk, I know exactly where the nanoweapons are," Destro told his team. "You will break into the Pit and take them. With those weapons I will control the entire world!"

Ana, Storm Shadow, and the Vipers boarded a Typhoon gunship and took off.

"You previously failed to get the weapons," Storm Shadow told Ana. "But this time we will succeed!"

Ana nodded. "Duke and his comrades can't stop us this time," she said.

The Typhoon landed a short distance from the Pit. As its main hatch dropped open, the Viper soldiers rushed out, followed by Ana and Storm Shadow.

Using a remote-control device, Ana activated a drilling machine known as a Mole Pod. The giant drill rolled out of the gunship and down a ramp.

When it reached the outer wall of the Pit, the Mole Pod began drilling.

"We're making our own entrance," Ana said. "We'll be inside in no time!"

CHAPTER THREE

A few minutes later the Mole Pod drill burst through the outer wall.

"We're in!" Ana shouted.

Ana, Storm Shadow, and the Vipers scrambled through the large hole. Within seconds they stood inside the Pit.

"Destro said that the weapons are being kept in the vault," Ana said. "And the only way to open the vault is with General Hawk's help. Come, let's pay the general a visit!"

Destro's agents moved silently as they made their way to General Hawk's office.

The general was shocked to see them, and before he could call for help, three Vipers seized him.

Ana grabbed the general's security badge and swiped it across the lock of the vault door.

Then Storm Shadow dragged the general up to the eye scanner. The scanner swept across his eye and the vault door swung open.

Ana rushed into the vault. There, on a table, was the weapons case.

"It's ours!" Ana snarled as she grabbed the case. "Now all we have to do is make our way out. Piece of cake."

Angered by the attack, General Hawk lunged desperately for an alarm button on his desk.

CHAPTER FOUR

BA-WHOOP! BA-WHOOP! BA-WHOOP!

Duke, Ripcord, Heavy Duty, and Scarlett were working out in the Pit's training room when the alarm suddenly blared.

"The nanomite weapons!" Duke shouted. "Let's move!"

The G.I. JOE agents sprang into action, racing from the training room.

THE BATTLE

As soon as the alarm sounded, Ana, Storm Shadow, and the Vipers raced from the vault. Ana clutched the weapons case in her hand.

They soon came to a series of catwalks running across the Pit. As Ana and Storm Shadow stepped out onto an upper catwalk, a blast shook the base.

THOOM! Heavy Duty blasted the upper catwalk. One end of the catwalk fell. Using his ninja skills, Storm Shadow easily leaped off.

Still holding the weapons case tightly, Ana slid down the falling catwalk and landed on the gangway below. Duke was there waiting for her.

"Hello, old friend," Ana said to Duke.

"If you're working for Destro now, you're no friend of mine," Duke replied. "Put the case down, Ana."

"No way, soldier boy," Ana said. "You may have stopped me last time. But this time the weapons are mine!"

Just then a Viper tackled Duke, sending him tumbling to the catwalk. Ana dashed away with the weapons.

Duke was struggling against the Viper when Ripcord drove a forklift loaded with metal plates onto the catwalk.

"Hang on, buddy! Here comes the cavalry!" Ripcord shouted.

Using whatever strength remained, Duke held off the Viper. Ripcord slammed into the Viper with the forklift, and the supersoldier fell off the catwalk.

CHAPTER FIVE

Ana ran along a lower catwalk. Then, from out of nowhere, Scarlett slammed into her, feet first. Ana fell hard, the weapons case flying out of her hand and onto a platform below.

Ana quickly jumped to her feet to fight off Scarlett.

“You’re not getting past me,” Scarlett boasted as she struck Ana with a roundhouse kick.

Ana ducked and returned a powerful kick of her own. “No one will keep me from taking those weapons!”

The battle in the Pit raged on with tremendous force. Scarlett continued to battle Ana. Duke, Heavy Duty, and Ripcord squared off against Storm Shadow and the Vipers.

Weapons' fire flew everywhere. Ninja swords flashed. And the G.I. JOE team was determined to keep the nanomite weapons from being stolen.

While his teammates were fending off G.I. JOE, Storm Shadow spotted an arclight jetpack hanging on a nearby wall. He strapped it on and took to the air, before swooping down to grab Ana.

"Thanks for the rescue," Ana said, "but we still need—"

"I know," Storm Shadow said. "Hang on."

Storm Shadow streaked through the air. He headed down to where the weapons case lay.

"Grab it!" he called out as he flew close.

Ana reached down and snatched the weapons case. "Got it!" she cried. "Let's go!"

MARS

Storm Shadow zoomed away from the G.I. JOE soldiers.

The G.I. JOE team gave chase, but they didn't stand a chance. A few seconds later Ana and Storm Shadow were out of the Pit.

"We did it!" Ana exclaimed.

Storm Shadow and Ana flew up to the closing doors of the Typhoon gunship. As soon as the two were on board, the aircraft took off into the desert night, heading for Destro's base.

Ana contacted Destro. His image immediately appeared on the Typhoon's view screen.

"We have the weapons," she reported proudly.

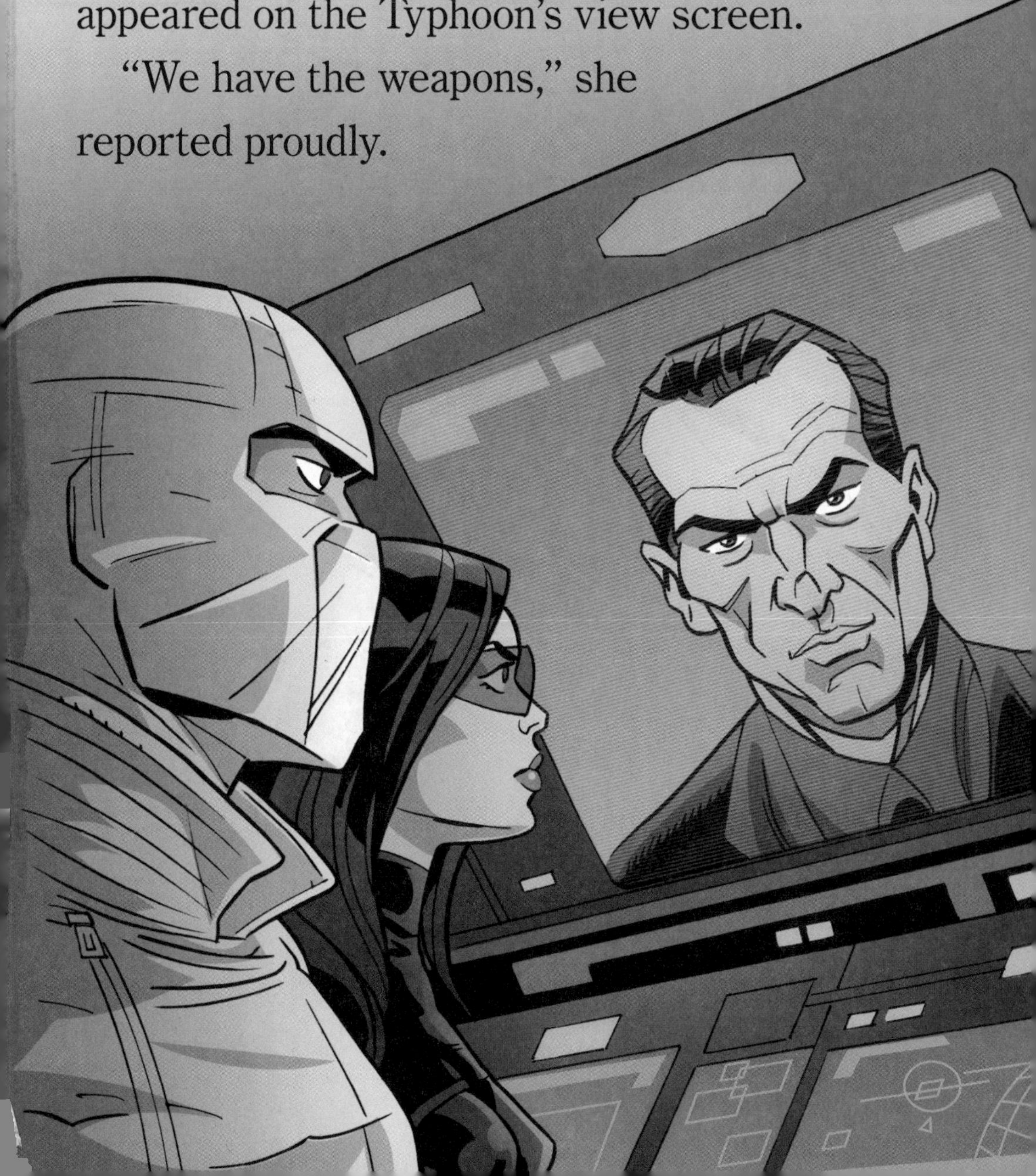

Destro smiled. “Now no one can stop me!” he said, laughing.

No one, of course, except G.I. JOE!